Mittens to Share

Emil Sher

illustrated by
Irene Luxbacher

North Winds Press
An Imprint of Scholastic Canada Ltd.

The artwork for this book was rendered in acrylics, graphite, charcoal and found papers and assembled digitally.

Library and Archives Canada Cataloguing in Publication

Sher, Emil, 1959-, author
Mittens to share / Emil Sher ; illustrations by Irene Luxbacher.
ISBN 978-1-4431-4296-0 (hardback)
I. Luxbacher, Irene, 1970-, illustrator II. Title.
PS8587.H38535M58 2016   jC813'.54   C2016-901030-9

www.scholastic.ca

6 5 4 3 2 1   Printed in Malaysia 108   16 17 18 19 20

For John, Becca, Stella and Sophie,
and the nests they weave
— E.S.

For Clemente, Luca, Juniper
and Deep River
— I.L.

Look up.

Look down.

Snow falling on the ground.

Snow, snow,
snow, snow.
Snowsnowsnowsnowsno—

Oh no!
One mitten.
Two hands.
Lost-mitten tears.

Out of the cold,
into the warmth.

Look inside the mitten box.

Grown-up mittens.

Outgrown mittens.

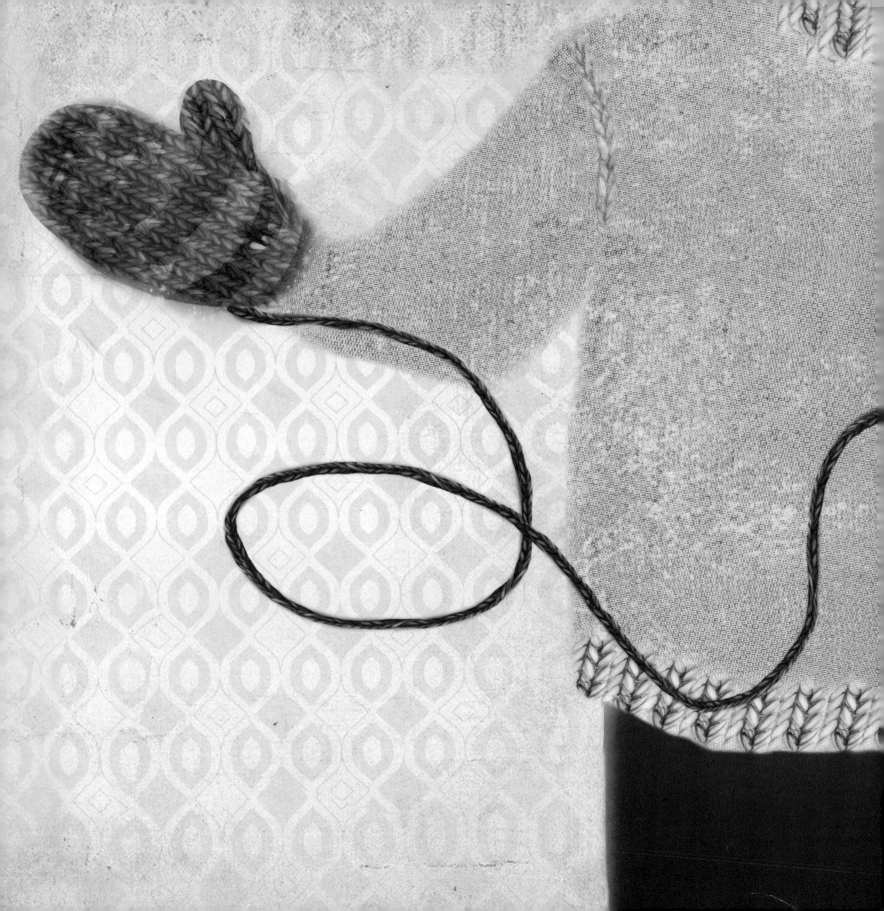

Fuzzy, warm
best-friend mittens.

Mitten mound.

Mitten mountain.

A big-enough-for-two mitten!

Out of the warmth.

Into the cold.

"Over there!"

A lost-and-found smile.
A mitten to share.